far away island
lake dog-a-bone
blue sky stage
PWL

To my dearest Sandy, thanks for always believing! —BF

"You've Just Gotta Believe!"

—Paddywhack Lane

Published by Paddywhack Lane Press.
Paddywhack Lane Press is an imprint of Paddywhack Lane LLC., Parker, Colorado 80138 USA.
Paddywhack Lane is a registered trademark of Paddywhack Lane LLC. (USA)

www.paddywhacklane.com

ISBN 978-1-936169-01-6

10 9 8 7 6 5 4 3 2 1

First Edition

Printed in China.

The COSTUME TRUNK

BOB FULLER

Courtney's big day was finally here!
"Make a special wish." said Rachel.
"I wish I was a royal princess!" said Courtney.

Later, everyone went outside to play.
"Be back before dark!" said Courtney's mother.

BIRTH

"Let's play pirates on the high seas," said Anthony.
"Aye, aye, captain. I'll be Joshua, the salty sea dog!" said Joshua.

The girls were not very excited about that idea.

Anthony turned to look for Courtney. “Hey, where’s she going?” he said.

“Maybe she wants to play Hide and Seek?” said Lauren.
Courtney was chasing her runaway balloon into the trees.

When the kids found Courtney,
she was staring up at a tall tree.
"Look! It's an old treehouse!" said Courtney.
They climbed the ladder and went inside.

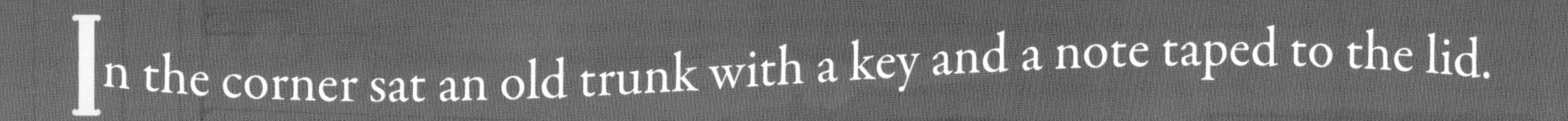

In the corner sat an old trunk with a key and a note taped to the lid.

Courtney unlocked the trunk, and opened the lid...

Lane, you can be
anything you want
to be, you've just
gotta believe!

SWO-O-O-OSH! Sparkles burst from the trunk.
Courtney stood on a stool, and lowered herself inside.
The lid closed above her, and then reopened.
When she climbed from the trunk, she was
wearing a beautiful princess costume.

"You look amazing!" said Rachel.
"Just like a real princess!" said Anthony.
"Excellent choice!" said Emily.
Courtney looked puzzled. "But, I didn't
choose anything. I think it chose me!" she said.

One by one, they each took a turn inside the trunk.

"Aaargghh! Ahoy mateys!" said Anthony.

"Woof!" barked Joshua.

Soon, the room was full of costumed kids.

Anthony and Joshua were playing pirate ship. "I wish we had a *real* boat," said Anthony.

Suddenly, the trunk opened... Again!

Anthony jumped inside. "Are you coming?" he said.

"Wait for me!" said Joshua.

Ella watched Anthony and Joshua disappear into the trunk.

"Come on girls, let's go!" said Ella. Courtney was last in line.

She pulled the note from her pocket, and read it again. "I believe!" she said.

Courtney climbed into the trunk, as the lid closed above her.

Instantly, Courtney found herself standing
in the most wonderful place she had ever seen!
Emily and Madeline called to her. "Courtney! Come over here!"

PWL
BLUE SKY STAGE
Paddywhack Lan

Emily and Madeline led Courtney to Cuddles Pet Place.

"I've always wanted a pony," said Emily.

"I'm teaching him to play fetch," said Madeline.

The girls played... until it was naptime.

"Hey! Over here! In the garden!" Lauren and Rachel yelled.

Courtney, Madeline and Emily ran to meet them.

"Have you ever seen such beautiful wildflowers?" said Lauren.

Rachel was busy watering, when she heard

music coming from the hills behind her.

"Do you hear that?" she said.

Courtney looked up as Ella pirouetted gracefully across the stage.

"Ella always dreamed of being a ballerina!" said Courtney.

"Wow! I never knew Chloe could sing like that?" said Rachel.

When the song ended, the kids clapped and cheered!

Next, everyone walked to a a bone-shaped lake in the valley below.

"Climb aboard, we're headed to the other side of the lake!" called Joshua.

When they reached the middle of the lake, scary waves rocked the boat.

Captain Anthony and his first mate, Joshua, guided them safely to the shore.

Walking along a path, Courtney saw a castle perched atop a high mountain peak.

"Who do you suppose lives there?" said Joshua.

"Must be somebody pretty special," said Ella.

"I sure wish it was mine!" said Courtney.

After a long hike, they reached the castle door.

Before Courtney could knock, the door opened...

A princess throne sat in the center of a magnificent party room.

For the rest of the afternoon, Courtney and her friends played games and enjoyed delicious cake and strawberry tea.

"This has been the best day ever!" said Courtney.

Suddenly, Courtney noticed the setting sun through the window.

"Hurry everyone, we need to get home!" she said.

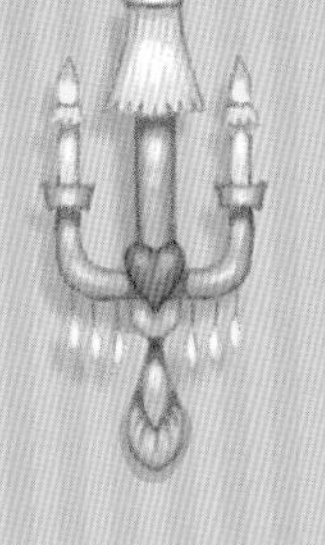

They ran down the path, around the lake and over the hills to the treehouse in the middle of Paddywhack Lane.

“Hey! What’s the trunk doing here?” said Ella.

“The trunk is our way back home.” said Courtney.

With that, everyone climbed inside and the lid closed.

Seconds later, the kids found themselves back in the old treehouse, behind Courtney's house. Just then, Courtney heard her mother's voice. "Courtney! It's time to come inside." she said. Courtney hugged her friends, and headed home.

Courtney's mother tucked her in, and kissed her on the cheek.
"Did you enjoy your special day, Sweetheart?" her mother asked.
"More than I could have hoped or wished or dreamed!" said Courtney.

Nearly everyday after their first visit, Courtney and her friends played in Paddywhack Lane, dressed in wonderful costumes, and had the most amazing adventures you could ever imagine!

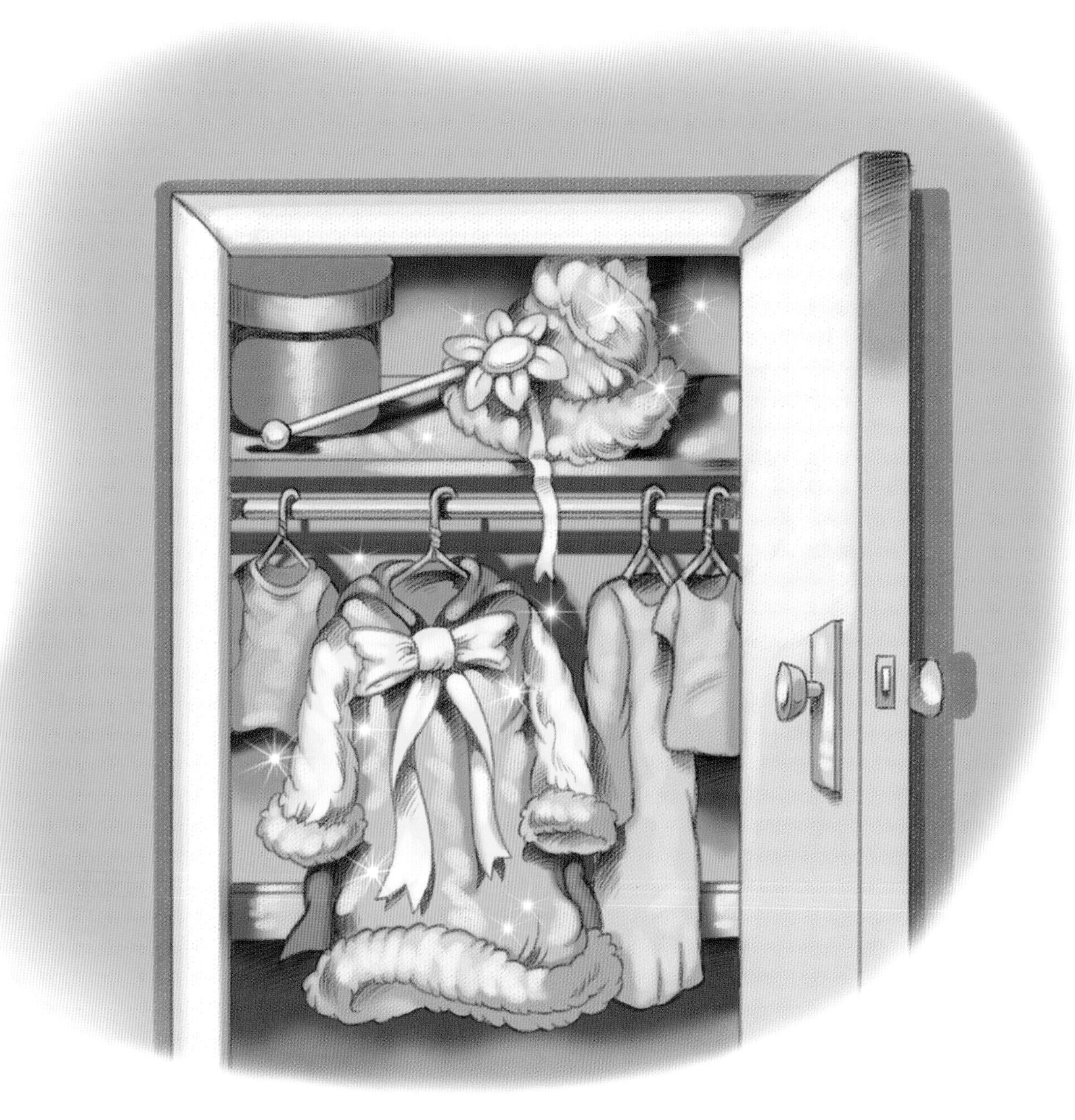

The Land of
Paddywhack Lane®

tower mountain

tall tree forest

sunshine garden

costume clubhouse

cuddles pet place

PETS